My Magical Pony

Silver Mist

Chapter One

"Drifter is really cool!" Carrie Jordan told Krista.

Krista was working with the lively little chestnut pony. She had him on the end of a long lunge line, trotting him round the arena. "*All* ponies are cool!" she grinned.

Drifter held his head high. He was enjoying this work, going from trot to canter and back to trot.

"When can I ride him?" Carrie wanted to know. She was new at the stables, and had only been riding for a few months.

My Magical Pony

Krista slowed the pony to a walk and let him stop beside Carrie. "Not until he's properly schooled and we can be sure that he's not going to take off with his rider again." *Once is enough,* she thought.

She remembered the time, a few weeks earlier, when Nathan Steele had snuck off with Drifter, then got lost and almost killed them both on the rocks at Black Point. It had taken Krista's magical pony to save them from the roaring waves.

A memory of Shining Star flying to the rescue broke Krista's concentration. He was so beautiful, with his long, silvery mane and shimmering white coat – a wonderful creature with broad wings, appearing in a glittering

Silver Mist

mist, always ready to help people in trouble.

"Good boy, Drifter!" Krista whispered now, patting his warm neck. The pony nuzzled her hand, looking for treats.

"Come on, let's give you a good brush-down and a nice juicy carrot," she smiled.

Carrie opened the arena gate to let Krista and Drifter out. "How long will it be before I can ride him?" she pestered.

"Ask Jo." Krista led Drifter into the stable yard and tied him up outside his stable.

Carrie dashed off to talk to Jo, the owner of Hartfell stables, leaving Krista to brush Drifter's long mane and tail and tell him how well he'd worked.

"Don't worry," she whispered to the pony. "Jo won't let Carrie ride you until she's had loads more lessons."

Drifter cocked his ears and tossed his head as if he understood every word.

"Just ask Shandy here," Krista went on, reaching out to stroke the old dark bay pony who had poked her head over her stable door. "Jo's great, isn't she?"

Shandy leaned over and nuzzled Drifter's

face. Since Drifter had arrived at Hartfell earlier that summer, the two ponies had become good friends.

"Good work, Krista," Jo said, striding across the yard. "Now could you tack up Shandy, Comanche and Misty, ready for a hack? You can leave Drifter in his stable with a hay net until after lunch, then put him out in the top field."

Saturday morning was a busy time on the yard. Cars were pulling up and dropping off kids, while Jo and Krista found saddles and bridles for the ponies. Today, however, they had extra help from Jo's friend, Rob Buckley.

Krista knew that Rob lived in Whitton,

7

but had spent time working in a trainer's yard
in Ireland. He was small and wiry, with grey
eyes and wavy fair hair.

By ten o'clock, eight riders and horses,
including Nathan Steele on Misty, were ready
to leave.

"Jo says I can't ride Drifter until next year,"
a glum Carrie told Krista as they left the yard
and walked steadily up to the bridleway.
She looked smart in her new hard hat and
cream jodhpurs – a pretty girl with a round,
sunshiny face and big blue eyes. She rode
Shandy, close behind Krista on Comanche.

"Hey!" Krista told her. "Just enjoy the ride,
why don't you?" How could you not, when
the moor was bright yellow with gorse, the

sun was shining and you could see for miles?

They rode on, over Hartfell and down into the next valley, keeping to the tracks and heading for the sands of Whitton Bay. Krista sat tall in the saddle, keeping Comanche on a loose rein, listening to conversations as they picked their way down the steep hillside.

"... I need some new riding boots, but Dad says they're too dear ... My cat just had four kittens ... so cute! ... It's a mystery. Mum read about it in the paper."

"Hey, Krista, did you hear that?" Nathan asked, reining Misty back and waiting for her to catch up.

"Did I hear what?"

"About the three horses that went missing from a field near Whitton."

"No. When?"

"Two weeks ago. The owners were on holiday, so a neighbour was looking after them. The police say they might have been stolen."

Silver Mist

"Poor things!" Krista frowned. She pictured the frightened horses being rounded up and forced into a horse-box, then driven off by strangers.

But she snapped back into the present when Rob rode by on Scottie. Krista decided to keep up with them as the hill levelled off and they stepped out on to the wide open beach of Whitton Sands. Comanche pricked his ears at the sound of the waves.

"Let's canter," Rob said to the group of riders.

Krista sat deep in the saddle and squeezed her piebald's wide sides. Comanche responded with a flick of his tail and a whinny. A split second later, they were charging along the beach towards the sea.

Chapter Two

A few hours after the ride, Krista cycled home.

She'd had a great day, starting with Drifter in the arena, followed by the exciting trek out to the beach, then chores back at the stable yard. Her arms and shoulders ached from mucking out, her pale blue T-shirt was grubby, her brown curly hair tousled by the wind. But it was the gallop along the sands that she was thinking about as she pedalled up the cliff path to her magic spot.

Comanche had been wonderful. He was a

gutsy, sturdy little pony with a cheeky look and lots of get-up-and-go. And he loved the beach. He'd ploughed into the white waves and raised a spray with his thundering hooves. The wind had caught his mane and sent it flying back, his neck stretched forward, his tail streaming behind.

Cool! Krista smiled to herself at the memory. She stopped at the crest of the hill. *I'm on top of the world! I'm the luckiest kid around!*

A gentle breeze ruffled her hair and cooled her warm face. It blew from the west, where the sun was sinking, and with it came a mysterious beating of wings.

Krista held her breath. Maybe – just maybe – Shining Star would appear today.

13

The breeze blew harder.

Please! Krista begged, gazing into the blue sky for the telltale signs of her magical pony. She longed to see a silvery cloud float across the face of the setting sun, to hear the wing beats grow louder, and for the beautiful white creature to appear.

"… I'm here!" a voice promised.

"Where?" Krista turned on the spot, looking out to sea, and up the steep fellside. It was his soft, wise voice – her very own Shining Star!

"All around you, waiting, watching."

"Do you need me?" she asked, turning again and again, until she began to feel dizzy on the narrow path.

"Not yet," the magical pony told her.

"But won't you let me see you?" One glimpse of his proud head and beautiful silky mane would be enough.

"Soon," he promised.

Then the breeze died away and the invisible wings stopped beating, and Krista knew that Silver Star had flown away.

"Did you have a good day?" Krista's mum asked.

Her dad had made a barbeque in the yard at High Point Farm. Krista could smell the burgers cooking. "I'm starving!" she exclaimed.

"Wash your hands!" her mum reminded her.

Dumping her bike, Krista zoomed into the kitchen, ran the tap and whisked her hands under it.

"Properly!" her mum insisted.

Krista groaned and grabbed some soap. Ten seconds later, she was back out in the yard.

"Good day?" her dad asked, turning the burgers one last time and making them sizzle.

"Cool!" she nodded. "We galloped on the beach." *I almost saw my magical pony!* She didn't say this last bit because Shining Star was a big secret that she kept to herself.

Soon she was biting into a huge burger sandwich and her mouth was too full to talk.

Later though, while her mum and dad

stayed by the barbie with some friends who had called round, Krista wandered around the back of the house, to the small, sloping garden overlooking the sea.

"This is for you, Spike!" she murmured to her pet hedgehog, putting down a dish of bread dipped in milk.

Then she sat on the grass and waited.

Soon Spike emerged from a hedge of prickly hawthorn. He waddled eagerly towards the dish and began chomping noisily.

"Guess what – I nearly saw Shining Star again today!" Krista whispered.

Chomp-chomp-gulp. Spike was busy with his feast.

"I heard him!" she confided. "So he's definitely still around."

Snort-slurp.

"It's ages since we rescued Drifter and Nathan from Black Point," she sighed. "I want to climb on Star's back and fly again, to look down and see our tiny house, to swoop over the sea and soar over the hill!"

For a moment Spike stopped guzzling,

cocked his head sideways and looked as if he was listening. *I hear you!* he seemed to say.

"You see, he only comes when someone's in trouble," Krista gabbled. "There's this amazing cloud of glittery dust, and giant wings beat, and a shape appears inside the cloud, like magic. That's Shining Star – inside a silver mist – and he asks me to save someone, and then he flies me off somewhere, and I help him, like I did with Nathan ..."

"Krista, who are you talking to?" Her dad interrupted.

She gasped. How long had he been there? What had he overheard?

"Hmm, there's only Spike here." Krista's dad looked puzzled. "I could've sworn you

19

were having a proper conversation."

"Yes, with Spike," she insisted. "I was telling him about my day."

Her dad laughed. "Typical Krista – chattering away to the animals!"

"Spike understands!" she grinned, jumping up and grabbing her dad's arm.

"Come on and have another burger," he said with a smile. "There's plenty left over."

"Cool!" she agreed.

She went happily, sure that her dad hadn't heard her secret, looking forward to tomorrow and another great day at the stables.

Chapter Three

"This is a big chance for Apollo," Jo told Krista, who had arrived at Hartfell early on Sunday morning.

Together they were getting the tall grey horse ready to travel in the horsebox. Krista wrapped his tail tightly in a bandage, while Jo fastened padded travel boots around his legs.

Apollo stood patiently in his stable, enjoying the attention.

"How long will you be away?" Krista asked.

"Five days altogether. Today I drive him up to Yorkshire. The competition starts tomorrow and goes on for three days. Then we drive back home on Thursday."

"Hey, Apollo, I'll miss you," Krista sighed. She slid his travel rug over his back and fastened the straps under his belly. "But you're going to do really well, I know it!"

"Cross country is his strongest event," Jo said. "He practically flies over the fences."

Krista nodded. "I wish I could see you."

"Maybe you can come with us next summer," Jo smiled.

She led Apollo out into the yard, where Rob was ready with the horsebox. He'd lowered the wide ramp and was standing by.

"This is the bit Apollo doesn't like," Jo warned.

The thoroughbred's head had gone up. He flattened his ears and flared his nostrils.

Krista nipped ahead with a bucket of food to tempt him inside the box. "Here, 'Pollo!" she murmured. "C'mon, that's a good boy!"

Gradually Jo led the horse on to the ramp. At first he shied at the hollow sound of his hooves on the board, then inched forward.

Krista showed him the food. "Here, boy!"

At last he overcame his fear and went in.

Rob raised the ramp from behind and closed the door. Krista hitched his headcollar to the trailer tie, then she and Jo left by the narrow side door.

23

"Good job!" Jo nodded.

She, Rob and Krista checked the door bolts then Jo climbed into the driver's seat.

"Good luck!" Krista told her.

"And don't worry about anything here," Rob ordered. Jo was leaving him in charge of the yard while she was  away. "If I need to know something, I can always ask Krista!"

Krista smiled. It was cool to feel important.

"OK, I'm out of here!" Jo nodded, turned on the engine and eased the horse-box towards the gate.

"Good luck!" Krista and Rob called again.

Then, with a wave, Jo and Apollo were gone.

It was later in the day, after Rob had taken out a trail ride and returned with all the ponies and riders safe, that Krista decided to work again with Drifter.

"Can I lunge him this time?" Carrie begged, following close on Krista's heels.

Krista sighed. Carrie was hard to shake off, but she was mad keen on Drifter, so Krista gave in. "You can help. I'll hold the lunge rein and you flick the whip in the air. The sound of the whip makes him trot on, but don't touch him with it whatever you do!"

Quickly Carrie figured out what to do. She grinned as she and Krista worked the little chestnut into a trot and then a canter.

"Excuse me!" A woman's voice interrupted the training session. "I'm looking for the yard owner."

Krista drew in the lunge rein then turned. "Jo's away for a few days," she answered.

The woman looked annoyed. She was

smartly dressed in a pale blue jacket and skirt, wearing her long blonde hair loose over her shoulders. "So who's in charge?" she asked loudly.

"That'd be me," Rob replied, striding towards the arena. He must have spotted the visitor from the tack room, where he'd been working. "How can I help?"

The blonde woman turned her back on Krista. "I want riding lessons."

"Well, you've come to the right place," Rob smiled. "But, as Krista said, the owner is away. It would be best to come back next weekend."

"How many horses do you have here?" Ignoring Rob, the woman headed back to the yard and began poking her head into the stables.

"Jo has twelve ponies and horses altogether," Rob explained.

"How many of them are little kiddy rides?"

Talk about rude! Krista frowned.

"There are eight ponies, all under thirteen hands, plus two Welsh cobs, a hunter called Major and this ex-racehorse, Scottie." Proudly Rob showed the woman the chestnut gelding with the white blaze down his face. "Then, of course, Jo has her own thoroughbred, who isn't here right now."

The woman seemed keen to know more about Scottie. "You say he's an ex-racehorse. What's his pedigree?" she asked.

"She doesn't even look like the type who would enjoy riding!" Krista muttered to

Carrie, glancing at the visitor's suit and high heels. The woman was nosey, and her loud voice got on Krista's nerves.

She was ready to start work with Drifter again, when she felt the wind suddenly change direction. "Huh!" she murmured.

"What?" Carrie asked.

Krista shook her head. "Nothing."

But she stood still and listened to a rustling sound – more than just the breeze disturbing the grass in the field beyond the arena, like a bird flapping its wings and rising into the air.

Again! Krista thought. She gazed into the sky, looking for the silver mist that would signal the arrival of her magical pony.

She saw white clouds high in the sky,

but they didn't glitter or sparkle, and Shining Star did not appear.

"Come on, Krista!" Carrie insisted.

Something's wrong! Krista said to herself. She knew for sure that the breeze and the sound of wings meant that Star was nearby.

"I'll be back!" the visitor told Rob after she'd finished quizzing him. She got into her car, slammed the door and drove off.

"Weird!" Krista muttered. As the rude woman drove off down the lane, the breeze died down and Krista no longer heard wings beating overhead.

"Krista, are we gonna do some more work with Drifter, or not?" Carrie demanded.

Frowning, Krista forced herself to forget

the visitor and the warning that her magical pony seemed to be giving her. *I probably made it all up!* she thought. *Nothing's wrong. I just didn't like the woman, that's all.*

"Trot on, Drifter!" she said, letting out the lunge rein.

Beside her, Carrie flicked the long whip.

The young pony picked up his feet and trotted smartly around the arena.

The moment had passed. *Back to normal!* Krista thought.

Hidden by the white clouds on the hillside, Shining Star watched and waited.

Chapter Four

At three o'clock Jo called Rob to tell him that she and Apollo had arrived safely.

"How did Apollo travel?" Krista quizzed him as soon as he came off the phone. "Was he all sweated up?"

"Jo says he was fine," Rob reported. "He was tucking into his hay net even as we spoke!"

Krista smiled and went on cleaning bridles. She and Rob were in the tack room, putting everything in order after another busy day. "I hope he wins. Wouldn't that be cool?"

Silver Mist

Rob lifted saddles on to the saddle rack, checking that the stirrups were neatly looped up. "Don't get your hopes up too high. Apollo's good, but maybe not that good," he warned.

Just then, Carrie poked her head through the door. "Can I give Drifter a carrot?" she asked.

Rob grinned. "Don't you have a home to go to?"

"Yep. Dad's waiting for me in the Land Rover, but can I feed this to Drifter before I leave?"

"OK, he's out in the top field with Scottie and Comanche. While you're up there, check that the gate is padlocked, would you?"

Carrie nodded quickly and disappeared.

"Which reminds me ..." Krista muttered. She knew that this was the time when Jo would normally check the row of padlock keys hanging from hooks next to the bridles. Red, yellow, blue, green – she went carefully through the coloured tags to see that they were in place.

"Good thinking," Rob said. "They say lightning never strikes twice, but you can't be too careful."

Krista gave him a puzzled frown.

"What I mean is,

I was in charge of those three horses at Bay
View when the owners were away."

"The ones that were stolen?" Krista gasped.

Rob nodded. "It happened out of the blue.
I wasn't staying at their house, but I'd been
down there during the day, checking that the
horses had water and that everything was
OK. That same night, the thieves came. The
police think they backed their vehicle into
the gate and tore it off its hinges. In the
morning, all three horses had vanished."

Krista felt a knot of worry tighten in her
stomach. "Will there be anyone here tonight
to keep watch?" she asked.

Rob nodded. "Don't worry – this time I'm
staying in the house while Jo's away."

"Cool." Relieved, Krista hung up the last bridle. It was time to go home. "See you tomorrow," she told Rob.

"Ponies, ponies, ponies – is that all you ever think about?" Krista's mum exclaimed over breakfast next morning.

"Yes!" Krista grinned.

It was two weeks in to the summer holidays, and so far Krista had spent every single day at Hartfell. Today was going to be no different.

"Do you want a lift to the stables?" her dad offered. He drove past them on his way to work.

Krista nodded, grabbed her toast and followed him into the yard.

Silver Mist

"Remember to pick her up on your way back," her mum told her dad as she waved goodbye.

Krista relaxed as her dad drove along the narrow lanes. She enjoyed looking up at the sky and watching the seagulls soar overhead. In the distance, the sea glinted. Close by, the fuchsia hedges were bright red with bell-shaped flowers. As they drew near to Hartfell, Krista spotted ponies' heads poking over the fences. "Hi, Shandy ... Drifter ... Misty ... Comanche ..." she greeted them one by one.

"Phew!" she said, jumping out of the car as soon as it stopped at the gate. She saw Rob wheeling a barrow across the yard. "Everyone's still here!"

"You bet!" he called back.

And then there was no time to think as Krista got stuck in. First she mucked out with Rob, then helped saddle the ponies. The morning was gone before she knew it.

After lunch, she groomed Scottie, then hosed down the yard. Finally, she went into the straw barn, climbed high among the bales and chose the one she wanted to make fresh beds for the horses.

"Watch out!" she yelled to Carrie, who had arrived early for her four o'clock lesson with Rob.

The straw bale tumbled down the stack and landed safely at Carrie's feet. Together they hauled it on to a wheelbarrow and

trundled it across the yard.

"I just had a call from Jo," Rob informed them as he came out of the tack room. "Apollo is in third place after the dressage!"

"Wow, that's brilliant!" This was better than Krista had expected. And tomorrow was cross country – his strongest event.

Carrie and Rob left her to spread straw on the floor of Shandy's stable while they went into the arena. *Third!* she repeated to herself, feeling proud of Jo's wonderful horse. *And maybe tomorrow he'll move up to second, or even first!*

The straw smelled sweet and rustled underfoot. Some of it stuck to her T-shirt and jodhpurs. She brushed it off as she emerged into the sunshine.

"That's good, Carrie!" Rob called. "You're rising nicely to the trot. Now just loosen the reins – there's no need to pull on Shandy's mouth. Yep, that's better!"

Picking straw out of her hair, Krista wandered over to watch the lesson. Carrie was definitely improving, if only she would let go of her tight grip on the reins.

In any case, she was really keen, trotting nicely, with her back straight and looking directly ahead.

"No, no, you're still pulling too hard!" Rob warned from his position in the centre of the arena.

Shandy tossed her dark head. The pressure of the bit in her mouth made her kick out with her back legs, tipping Carrie forward.

"Don't panic!" Rob said as Carrie dropped the reins and grabbed the front of the saddle.

Uh-oh! Krista thought. *She's lost her balance, she's coming off — yes, she's falling!*

Thud! Carrie landed in a heap.

Rob ran towards her while Krista vaulted the fence and tried to catch Shandy.

Once she'd cornered the pony and taken hold of her reins, she led her quickly out of the arena and across the yard to her stable.

After that, Krista dashed back to find out how Carrie was.

The girl was still lying on her back, but by now she was trying to sit up. She groaned and fell back.

"Take your time," Rob said. "What hurts?"

"My arm," Carrie whimpered.

"OK, let me take a look. Can you move your fingers – yes, that's good. Can you lift your arm?"

"Ouch!"

Krista watched as Rob gently helped Carrie to her feet.

"I don't think you've broken anything, but I'm going to take you to hospital in Whitton, just to be sure."

Carrie sniffed and did her best not to cry. She looked pale and shaky as Rob led her past Krista. "How's Shandy?" she managed to ask.

"She's fine. Don't worry about her."

"Krista, is it OK if I leave you here?" Rob asked. "Can you put Shandy out in the field with the others and then lock everything up for the night?"

Krista nodded. She held Rob's car door open as the injured girl got in. "I hope you'll be OK, Carrie."

"She'll be fine," Rob assured her. "I'll call her parents. They'll probably come to the hospital. I should be back in about an hour."

"No problem," Krista insisted.

She felt worried as she watched Rob drive Carrie down the lane, but she knew exactly what to do.

First she led Shandy out to the top field, to join Drifter and Scottie. Then she carefully

checked on the eight other ponies and horses in two other fields close to the stables. All were calmly grazing in the late afternoon sunshine.

The peaceful sight soothed Krista, and after checking the padlocks, she went back to the tack room to count the keys. Red for the tack room, blue for the long field, yellow for the near field … but the green tag for the top field was missing.

Hmm. Krista searched on the bench beneath the hooks, then on the floor. The key was lying in a dusty corner. *Phew!* She breathed a sigh of relief and hung the key on its hook. After a final glance at the rows of tack, she closed the door.

My Magical Pony

"Hi honey!" Her dad waved from their car which he'd parked in the lane. "Are you all finished here?"

Krista ran to meet him. "Yeah, but Carrie had an accident. Rob took her to hospital. I thought maybe I should wait until he gets back."

Her dad shook his head. "Sorry, Krista. I promised your mum that we'd be back by six o'clock. She wants us to visit your grandma tonight. That means we'd better get a move on."

Krista stood uneasily beside the car. She glanced back at the empty yard. All the stable doors were shut, the wheelbarrows were neatly lined up against a wall, and two grey pigeons preened themselves on the hay barn roof.

Silver Mist

"Come on, I'm sure Rob will be back soon," her dad insisted.

With a nod, Krista agreed. Of course everything would be all right.

She got into the car and her dad eased it into the lane. "Apollo came third in the dressage event," she told him. "I think he might get first in cross country. Wouldn't that be cool?"

Looking ahead to tomorrow, Krista dreamed of more silk rosettes for Jo to pin up on the tack room wall.

Chapter Five

That night Krista had a wonderful dream.

In the dream she was with Shining Star, soaring through a midnight sky. Her magical pony's great white wings were beating steadily, they were flying amongst the twinkling stars and Krista felt she could reach out and touch the pale gold disc of the moon. Behind them they trailed a fine silver mist.

"There is a great deal of sorrow in your world," her wise pony said, gazing down at the curved outline of her planet. "In Galishe, where I come from, all creatures are content."

"Can they fly, like you?" Krista asked.

"Only the ponies," he told her, gliding silently between the stars. "We are sent across the heavens to help those in trouble."

"And are they all as beautiful as you?"

"All," he said.

With a sigh Krista leaned forward and rested her head against the magical pony's neck.

"Krista?" A voice broke into the dream.

She woke and found herself standing in her pyjamas at her bedroom window.

"What are you doing?" her mum asked from the doorway. "I heard you get out of bed. It's one o'clock in the morning!"

Krista blinked hard. Her window was open and a warm breeze was coming in. "I was dreaming," she murmured.

"You've been sleep-walking," her mum said softly, taking her hand and leading her back to bed. "What was the dream about?"

"I was flying."

Her mum lifted the duvet and let her slide under it into her still warm bed. "Was it nice?"

"Mmmm."

"Shall I leave the curtains open?"

Krista snuggled deep under her duvet. She wanted to go back to sleep and fly through the night sky again. "Mmmm."

"Krista?" her mum said softly.

There was no reply.

"Here's your breakfast!" Krista told Spike early next morning. She'd got up before her mum and dad and taken her prickly pet a small dish of cat food, which he loved.

The little hedgehog pushed his snout into the dish and ate eagerly.

Inside the house, the phone began to ring. Krista scooted back to answer it.

"Hi, Krista, it's Jo," the voice on the other end of the line said. "Sorry to bother you so early, but I've been trying to get through to Rob and he's not answering his phone."

The news worried Krista. "Do you want me to give him a message? I can set off for the stables right now."

"No, it's not urgent. I was just wondering how things were at Hartfell. You can probably tell me as much as Rob can."

"I was there until teatime yesterday," Krista told her. She wondered whether to tell Jo about Carrie's fall then decided against it in case it put Jo off during her cross country event later that morning. "Rob had to go out, but he said he'd soon be back."

Silver Mist

"Yeah, I'm sure everything's fine," Jo said. "Apollo's doing well up here, did you know?"

"I heard," Krista replied. "Are you nervous about today?"

"No, I'm more worried about tomorrow and the show-jumping. That's when the pressure really gets to him."

"Good luck!" Krista told Jo that she would be thinking about them and willing them to win. "Give Apollo a hug from me!"

"He'd be more interested in a carrot, if I know him!" Jo joked. "Anyhow, I'm glad to hear that everything's OK at your end."

"Cool," Krista said, putting the phone down with a frown. She called upstairs to her mum and dad. "I'm off to the stables!"

Her dad popped his head out of the bathroom door. "Already?"

"Yep, I'll go on my bike. See you later."

Without waiting for him to object, Krista ran out of the house and set off on her bike. *Why wasn't Rob answering his phone?* she wondered, pedalling hard along the cliff path. *Maybe the battery went dead. Or else he left it in his car and didn't hear it.*

Still, she was anxious as she reached the high point on the path where Shining Star had first appeared. She paused for a moment to catch her breath. *Why didn't I wait at the yard until Rob got back?* she asked herself, gazing down at Whitton Bay. *I ought to have waited, I really ought!*

Silver Mist

Too late now, she decided. All she could do was to cycle on against the wind, down the hill and up again, on to the lane to Hartfell.

So far, so good! Krista stopped pedalling and climbed the fence to see into the long field.

She spotted Comanche and Misty, along with three other ponies, all busily grazing in the cool morning air.

My Magical Pony

Next along the lane was the near field,
with the two Welsh cobs, a Connemara mare
and Rusty the Shetland. The little pony was
pleased to see her and came trotting up on his
stumpy legs.

Krista smiled and gave his bony nose a
good rub. She pushed his forelock out of his
eyes and tidied his rough mane. "I have to go
and check the top field," she told him, leaving
him with his head peering over the hedge.

Krista reached the yard. *I'm sure I left the yard
gate closed,* she thought, cycling in and leaning
her bike against the barn wall. Then she
looked around for Rob's old grey Jeep.

Not here! Did that mean he hadn't
come back from Whitton after all? And had

the house been empty all night?

Krista's skin began to prickle and her heart to beat faster. She set off at a run towards the top field.

And what did she find? A gate off its hinges – a wide open expanse of grass!

"Oh no!" Krista cried, rushing through the gate. This was where she'd left Drifter, Shandy and Scottie safely locked in for the night.

She ran up the hill, almost tripping on the rough ground, then she turned and gazed around the empty field. *No ponies!*

"They've been stolen!" Krista whispered in disbelief.

Chapter Six

Krista's legs gave way and she sat down hard on the ground.

This is my fault! she thought. *Why didn't I wait for Rob to come back?*

Then other ideas rushed into her head. Perhaps the horses hadn't been stolen after all. Maybe they had crashed the gate and escaped by themselves.

In a fresh panic, Krista jumped up and began a new search – back through the stable yard and out to the lane, gazing down the steep slope of gorse and heather, then up to the rugged horizon behind Hartfell.

But the hills were deserted.

I should have waited for Rob! she told herself a second time.

Almost in tears, Krista went back to the tack room. She sat heavily on the bench beside the saddle racks, hardly noticing the sound of a car engine, then the slam of a door before Rob came to join her.

"Hey, what's wrong?" he asked.

She sat up straight and took a deep breath. "It's the horses in the top field," she managed to say, then shook her head, unable to go on.

"… It's *not* your fault!" Rob insisted.

He had sat down beside Krista and listened

to the full story. Now, though his face was solemn, he tried to make her feel better.

"If anything, it's down to me," he went on. "I didn't get back here at all last night, like I said I would."

"What happened?" Krista asked, drying her eyes.

"I took Carrie to hospital. They X-rayed her arm, which was badly sprained but not broken. But then they checked for concussion and decided she should stay in overnight."

"Is she OK?"

Rob nodded. "I rang Mr and Mrs Jordan and they came to the hospital. I had to stay with them for a while to explain what had happened."

"Were they upset?" Krista asked.

"Not too bad. But when I finally left Whitton to head back to Hartfell, it was late. Then I found I was low on fuel and there were no garages open, so I had to kip down for the night at my place, and I finally bought some diesel this morning and got back here."

"I knew I shouldn't have left yesterday teatime," Krista sighed. "It felt wrong."

"Like I say, it's not your fault." Rob walked from the tack room into the yard, hoping to see the missing ponies suddenly appear.

"I guess we'd better call Jo and tell her what's happened," he sighed.

"If we do, we'll ruin her chances of winning!" Krista protested. "No way will she be able to concentrate after she hears this."

"Hmm." Rob folded his arms. "It's a tough one. But if I were Jo, I'd want to know about Scottie and the others. If we tell her, then it's up to her whether she stays in Yorkshire for the competition or comes down here to help us find them."

"But maybe they'll turn up straight away." Krista was finding more reasons not to upset Jo. "Anyway, this is a really big chance for Apollo to get up to national level, and maybe even train for the next Olympics!"

Silver Mist

Rob walked away, his head hanging, deep in thought. "OK, we'll leave it until lunchtime," he decided at last.

"Yes!" Krista let out a sigh of relief. "So what do we do now? Shall I go back to the field and look for hoof marks and more clues like that?"

"Good idea, but don't touch anything," Rob agreed. He searched in his jacket pocket for his phone, then remembered. "The battery's dead," he explained to Krista. "Go ahead. You check the field."

"What about you?" she asked, feeling the panic rise again. "What are you going to do?"

"Phone the police," Rob answered, before he disappeared into the house.

Chapter Seven

When she looked hard, Krista found plenty of clues in the top field.

For a start, there were wide tyre marks in the soft ground at the entrance to the field. They showed that a heavy vehicle had stopped there – probably a horse-box or, more likely, a Land Rover with a trailer.

Krista studied the tyre marks, careful not to tread on them and scuff them with her boots. Then she noticed a piece of yellow plastic half hidden in the grass. She parted the grass and found that it was a corner from a car number plate.

I bet this came off the thieves' trailer! she thought, determined to show it to the police later on.

She went on searching and soon found a second clue. *What's this patch of churned-up turf?* she wondered, stepping over the tyre tracks and going into the empty field. She soon discovered that the mess had been caused by hooves, as if the ponies had struggled when the thieves tried to drag them into the trailer. Clods of earth had been torn up and trampled. There were skid marks and deep hoof prints, all in a jumble.

Krista shook her head. She was already feeling sick with worry, but then when she found her third clue, she had to take a deep breath and hurry away.

"There's blood on the gate post!" she told Rob in a desperate voice, running across the yard towards the house.

"Calm down," Rob said. "The police are on their way. They should be here any minute."

"I saw blood!" Krista insisted. "One of the horses must have been bleeding!"

"Or one of the thieves," he pointed out. "C'mon, Krista, let's not jump to conclusions."

"It was horrible," she sighed, convinced

that the blood belonged to Scottie, Drifter or Shandy. "The poor thing!"

Scottie, the fine chestnut thoroughbred with his long, slim legs, so easily damaged. Drifter, the highly strung young pony, liable to panic and hurt himself on a sharp edge. And Shandy – good, reliable old Shandy, so clever. Krista shuddered.

"I've cancelled today's lessons," Rob told her, "but I haven't been able to get in touch with Sean, the blacksmith. He's due here to shoe Misty at ten."

"I'll bring her in," Krista said, glad to have something to do while they waited.

She went out with a head collar and led the speckled grey pony back into the yard.

Rob greeted her there with the news that he'd taken a phone call from the Jordans, who had reported that Carrie was back home from the hospital and doing well.

"That's one good thing," Krista muttered, brushing Misty and picking out her feet, ready for Sean. "Stand!" she told her gently, trying not to let the grey pony know how

scared she was about the missing horses. She was glad to see the smith's blue van drive into the yard, just ahead of a police car with two policemen inside.

"What's up?" Sean asked Krista, parking next to the stone arch where all the horses were shod. "What's with the cops?"

The police officers slammed their car doors and met up with Rob by the tack room.

"We've lost three horses," Krista muttered. She didn't know Sean very well. He was tall, with jet black hair, and lived in the next village down the coast from Whitton.

"Bad news!" Sean shrugged, unloaded his tools and set his furnace going.

Then, between the clank and hammering

of metal, Krista listened in to Rob's conversation with the police.

"So there was no one here last night to look after the property?" one of the men said.

"I explained why," Rob told him. "We had an emergency here and I had to take a girl to hospital."

"But you stayed away all night." The other police officer frowned. "I take it you have someone who can back up your story?"

"Uh-oh!" Sean muttered under his breath, so that only Krista could hear. "Robbie had better watch what he says!"

"This isn't funny!" Krista murmured. She heard the sizzle of red hot metal as Sean plunged a horse shoe into a bucket of cold water. For a while, she couldn't overhear what else was being said by the police and Rob.

"… Your alibi seems pretty thin to me," the first police officer warned. "You're sure you didn't see anyone at all after you left the hospital at seven p.m., until you arrived here just before nine a.m.?"

"I went straight home," Rob insisted. "I live alone."

"Which left this place uncared for, even though you'd promised the owner – Miss …"

"Weston, Jo Weston," Rob told him.

"… Even though you'd promised Miss Weston that you'd be here."

Again Sean shook his head. "Big trouble!"

he warned, picking up Misty's front hoof and wedging it between his knees. Then he bent forward to nail the shoe in place.

Krista stood by the pony's head, dreading what was coming next.

"By the way, weren't you involved in the theft of those horses from Bay View?" the first man challenged. "Rob Buckley – I seem to remember your name coming up then."

Caught off guard, Rob gave a sickly grin. "What d'you mean, 'involved'? I was looking after them, if that's what you're saying."

"Funny, that!" the taller policeman said, without smiling.

"Look!" Rob began, but the first man cut in.

"I take it you've rung the owner and told

Silver Mist

her what's happened?"

Rob shook his head. "Not yet."

"Tut!" Sean clicked his tongue, seizing a second shoe from the furnace with a pair of long, heavy tongs. He still didn't seem to be taking the situation very seriously.

"That was my fault!" Krista hissed. "It was because I wanted Jo to do her cross country without worrying!" She felt her hands starting to shake as she held Misty's lead rope. It looked like the police were more than ready to blame Rob.

"I'd make that phone call now, if I were you," the first policeman said, walking with the other towards the top field. "We'll take a look at the scene of the crime."

Checking that Sean could manage without her, Krista ran after them. She caught them up by the gate.

"I found this!" she cried, showing them the piece of yellow number plate in the grass. "And this!" She pointed with a shaking hand to the bloodstain on the gatepost.

"There's definitely been some sort of

74

struggle," the tall man said, carefully picking up the sharp piece of plastic. He turned towards her. "And you are ...?"

"Krista. I'm the one who discovered that the horses were missing," she told him. "And Rob *did* have to take Carrie to hospital!" She stuck up for him as best she could.

The other man grunted. "Bit of a coincidence that he was around at the time of *both* thefts," he pointed out.

"But he wouldn't do anything to hurt the ponies!" Krista told them. "He's lived with horses all his life. Jo wouldn't have left him in charge if he wasn't ... if he couldn't be ..."

"Couldn't be what?"

"Couldn't be trusted," she said weakly.

A sudden doubt entered her head. After all, what did she really know about Rob Buckley?

And then she heard a faint voice in the wind. "I'm watching and waiting ... Krista, I'm ready to come when you call!"

Krista gasped and looked up at the sky. It was clear blue, and there was no breeze on her face. Had she really heard Shining Star speak her name?

"Listen, love, there's no need to get too upset," the taller policeman advised. "Why not go home for a while and let us sort this out for Miss Weston?"

"I'd rather stay," Krista told him.

"No, it's best if you're out of harm's way. Shall we get your parents to collect you?"

76

"Waiting!" Shining Star said again.

Where? she wondered. *I need you. Please come!*

"Krista?" the policeman prompted.

"What? Oh, no thanks. I can cycle back," she said quickly.

"Meet me at our magic spot!" Star whispered in the breeze.

Yes, a breeze! A soft wind had begun to blow. Krista was sure she could make out a silver mist blowing in from the sea.

"Make sure you go straight home," the policeman told her. "You've had a bit of a shock, you know."

Krista nodded again. Now she couldn't leave Hartfell soon enough.

She dashed from the top field, back to the

stable yard, where Sean had finished Misty's shoes and put her back in the field.

"Rob's still in the house, talking to Jo," the blacksmith told her.

"Tell him I had to go home!" Krista gabbled, picking up her bike and pedalling on to the lane. "I'll be back later, I promise!"

Sean called after her, but nothing would stop her from cycling on to the cliff path, along the narrow path overlooking Whitton Bay, towards the spot where she had first met Shining Star.

Chapter Eight

"Here I am!" Krista called, head tilted back, the wind blowing through her dark curly hair.

This was the magic place – on a high point along the cliff path, with the waves breaking on the rocks far below.

"Thieves have stolen Scottie, Drifter and Shandy. Please, Shining Star, you have to help us!"

"Meet me," he had told her. And his voice had been in the breeze at Hartfell. He must be here, at the magic spot.

Slowly a mist formed on the high horizon.

It began to roll down the rough moorland, drifting over the heather, into crevices between the rocks. A white mist gradually becoming silver, curling towards Krista.

"Thank you!" she breathed, closing her eyes for a moment. When she opened them again, Shining Star was beginning to emerge.

Krista made out his dark eyes and glorious silken mane, his arched neck and outstretched wings. The mist sparkled all around him.

"Here I am!" he said to her.

She nodded. "I'm so glad you came."

Tossing his head and folding his wings, Shining Star showered Krista with silver dust. "There is danger," he warned.

"Blood!" she told him. "There was a struggle.

Someone got hurt."

The magical pony's eyes gazed into hers.
"This is a harsh world," he said quietly, "where
innocent creatures are taken from their homes
and hidden away in dark, secret places."

"Do you know where they are?" Krista
cried. She breathed in the magic silver
mist, reaching out to touch Shining Star's
shimmering coat. His neck was warm and soft.

The pony shook his head. "There was a
fight. Fear in the air. A cry for help."

"Who did this?" Krista pleaded. "Who
would be so cruel?"

"We must find out," Shining Star agreed.
Then, in a voice more serious than she
had ever heard him use, he warned her.

"I see horses held prisoner in a place without water or food. No one goes there. There is no daylight, there is loneliness and despair."

"What shall we do?" Krista cried.

The magical pony spread his wings. "Climb on my back," he invited. "We will return to Hartfell."

She hesitated, under the shadow of the pony's great white wings. "The police are there. What if they see you?"

"They will see only a moorland pony like any other," he reminded her.

Krista nodded, knowing that no one else could see Shining Star's wings. She sat astride his back and held tight to his mane.

Shining Star began to beat his wings.

My Magical Pony

Krista felt the rush of wind as they rose from the ground. The earth slipped from under them and they seemed to enter a whirling tunnel of trees, rocks and heather. The sky was a pinprick of light in the distance, growing larger, glittering, turning silvery blue and then opening up above them.

She looked down. They were flying.

Everything was different.

Krista's magical pony soared over the sea, which glittered and sparkled in the sunlight. Tiny white boats bobbed on the blue water.

She glanced up. There was nothing but sky.

Shining Star's wings beat steadily up and down. He sailed across air currents, tilted his

wings and curved back towards the shoreline,
over the breaking waves and thin strip of pale
sand. Krista spied a row of bright beach huts,
small as dominoes, a few cars glinting on the
road running along the edge of Whitton Bay,
and then the moor rising up from the bay.

"There's Hartfell!" She pointed to a

rambling house set into the wooded hillside, surrounded by a few fields, so tiny that it looked like a child's toy farm.

As the magical pony swooped down, Krista felt her stomach lurch. They landed and she held tighter still to his mane, leaning forward to shield herself from the strong beat of his wings.

In the yard at Hartfell, Rob stood talking to Sean. There was no sign of the police car or of the two police officers.

Krista and Shining Star approached quietly from the lane.

The two men turned and spotted them.

"Hey, Krista, where did you find that little

guy?" Sean asked, noting the dappled grey pony which she rode bareback and without a bridle.

"On the cliff path," she replied. "I've ridden him before."

"He must be living wild up there," the blacksmith decided, too involved in his conversation with Rob to pay much attention.

"What happened with the police?"

"They went to check up on the letters on that piece of number plate you found by the gate," Rob told her, his face drawn. "I thought they were going to arrest me on the spot and throw me into jail!"

"And what about Jo?"

"I talked to her and convinced her to stay

where she is. Apollo got first place in the cross country. He's second overall right now."

"Cool!" Krista gasped. She sensed that Shining Star was listening hard and watching every movement Rob made. "She can't throw away a chance like that. But I bet she was worried about Scottie and the others."

"Yeah, she nearly lost it when I told her. But you know Jo – she's tough!"

"Guess what," Sean cut in. "She told Rob that Scottie's worth over five grand!"

"Five thousand pounds!" Krista echoed. "What about Drifter and Shandy?"

"Less. Probably around three thousand for Drifter and a couple of thousand for Shandy," Rob said. "That's ten altogether. Horse stealing is big business, when you add up what these animals are worth."

Standing in the yard with Krista on his back, Shining Star stamped his front hoof impatiently and turned towards the gate.

"Looks like we're off!" Krista told the two men, trying to sound casual. She waved as they headed back into the lane and up towards the top field. "What's wrong?" she asked Star.

The pony stopped by the gate. "Something was not right in the stable yard."

"Was it Rob?" she asked anxiously.

"I don't know. And here, there is danger," he warned, laying his ears flat and flaring his nostrils. "Cruel blows are raining down, horses are suffering …"

My Magical Pony

"Stop!" Krista pleaded.

Shining Star raised his head, seeing yet not seeing the entrance to the field where they stood. "It is night. The big chestnut horse is bleeding from a cut to his face."

"Scottie!" she murmured. "Can you see anything else?"

The pony shook his head. "Nothing but darkness."

Then Krista asked the question that had been spinning round inside her head. "You've just seen Rob. Do you think he's the thief?"

There was a long silence. A silver mist hung in the air above their heads as they stood by the open gate. "That's what we have to find out," Shining Star said.

Chapter Nine

Krista and Shining Star flew for a second time that day, through a dark rush of warm wind, out into a dawn of glittering silver light.

This time they landed at Bay View, a tall old house at the far end of Whitton Bay. The lonely house overlooked the sea and was surrounded by open fields.

"This is where the thieves stole the first three horses," Krista reminded Shining Star. "You can see how easy it is for a trailer to pull up here without anyone noticing."

"And they never found them?" the magical

pony asked. He pricked his ears and listened.

"No. They just vanished. I expect the thieves sold them for loads of money."

"Or else they're keeping them in a secret place until the fuss has died down and it's safe to sell them."

"Locked up like prisoners?" Krista frowned. For some reason, Shining Star seemed to think that the thieves hadn't got rid of any of the ponies.

"I can hear them," Star said mysteriously. "They are not far away! But these thieves are clever, Krista. They have hidden the horses well."

"What exactly can you hear?" she asked, sliding from his back and inspecting the field furthest from the house. It was empty. The grass was long and scattered with golden buttercups.

"Hooves stamping inside a dark metal box," Shining Star replied.

"That must be the trailer they used to steal the horses!"

"Men's voices shouting."

"The thieves! How many?"

"Two. And a lighter voice – a woman."

"That makes three. What else?"

"I can see trees. Many trees."

"A forest? Perhaps that's where they're hiding the horses." Krista trusted what Shining Star was telling her. With his magic sixth sense he could see and hear things that no ordinary being could. "All we have to do is find it!"

"An easy thing to say," Star warned her. "But hard to do."

"I wonder if Rob *was* in on it." Krista went off on a new tack. "Maybe we should check his story about staying late at the hospital."

Shining Star took up the idea. "We'll visit Carrie's family anyway," he decided. "Is their house far from here?"

"No. She lives in Whitton, down by the harbour. We can walk into town from here."

So they left Bay View and trotted along the quiet road into town, soon coming to more houses and a busier road leading down the hill towards the centre of town. Here Krista warned Star to slow down.

"Cars might not stop for us," she explained. "We have to be more careful."

And sure enough, a dark blue van whizzed past without slowing down. "Idiot!" Krista muttered, still frowning when a second car –

a flashy black, open top BMW with a woman driver – shot out from a side street and almost ran into them.

The woman gave a blast of her horn which sent Shining Star skittering sideways.

"Get that pony off the road!" the fair-haired woman shouted. "If you can't control him, you're not fit to be out!"

Krista was on the point of flinging back an answer about the woman's lousy driving when she recognized who it was. "I know her!" she muttered to Shining Star. "I've seen her before!"

By now the car was pulling away, heading out of town, but then stopping at traffic lights. Without waiting for Krista to explain, Star turned and followed it.

Silver Mist

"She came to Hartfell the other day," Krista told him. "She said she wanted lessons, even though she wasn't dressed for riding. Then she started poking around in the stables, asking Rob lots of questions about Scottie!"

The lights changed to green and the short queue of cars moved off.

"Keep after her!" Krista urged, quite sure now that this woman had been behaving suspiciously at Hartfell. After all, why had she been so interested in Scottie, and only a day before he'd been stolen!"

Shining Star trotted quickly after the black car, following it up a narrow country road then turning after it up a private lane until it reached a pair of wide iron gates – the entrance to a large estate.

"Wait!" Krista whispered, watching anxiously.

They saw the gates swing open and the car glide slowly through. Then the gates closed.

Krista and Shining Star walked closer. There was a name carved into the old stone gatepost – Oakwood Hall. A high wall to

either side blocked their view.

"What now?" Krista asked.

Shining Star pranced on the spot. "Nothing," he replied.

"What do you mean, 'nothing'?" Krista demanded. "We have to follow her!"

"How?" Shining Star looked up at the tall gates.

"You can fly over them!"

"No," he insisted.

"Why not?"

"Be patient," her magical pony said. "What do we know about this woman, except that she visited the stables?"

"And she's horrible to horses in traffic!" Krista muttered. But she could see that Star might be right.

"In any case, it's time to take you home," he insisted. "Look at the sun sinking in the west. The day is drawing to a close."

My Magical Pony

"Not yet!" she pleaded.

"Yes." Shining Star turned from the gate and spread his wings, preparing to fly. "Tomorrow we will search again."

"An awful thing has happened!" Krista's mum told her the moment she walked through the door of Highpoint Farm.

Krista's dad was home from work. They were both sitting at the kitchen table, waiting for the phone to ring.

"Tell me!" Krista urged. She'd said goodbye to Shining Star in the lane, promising to meet him again early next morning at the magic spot.

"Rob has been arrested," her dad said quietly. "We've left a message on Jo's phone.

We're expecting her to ring us back."

Krista sat down heavily at the table. "When did they arrest him?" she groaned.

"An hour ago," her dad said. "I saw Sean in town on my way home from work. He told me that the police have charged Rob with stealing the horses."

Slowly the news sank in, but Krista couldn't think of anything to say. Instead, she sat with her chin in her hands.

"They found some evidence," her mum went on. "Sean told your dad that the broken number plate from the thieves' trailer matched up with the registration on Rob's car."

Krista nodded. "That's bad. Did Rob tell them where the horses are?"

"No. He insists he doesn't know what the police are talking about," her dad told her. "He still says he was at the hospital, then drove straight home."

"Rob claims he's innocent," Krista's mum repeated after what seemed like an endless silence. She leaned across the table and took her daughter's hands between hers. "Honestly, love, I just don't know what to think!"

Chapter Ten

"Are you sure you don't want to come with us in the car?" Krista's dad asked after an early breakfast.

He and her mum were driving over to Hartfell to keep an eye on the place until Jo got back. After a long talk with Jo the night before, Krista's dad had taken time off work to help out.

"No thanks!" Krista was eager to be off.

"But you'll cycle over later?" her mum checked, finding it strange that Krista didn't want to dash over with them.

She nodded. "I want to visit Carrie and see how she is." *Plus, really, I have to go to the magic spot and meet Shining Star!*

Krista had hardly slept for worrying about the missing horses. She'd tossed and turned in bed, getting up to look out of the window in the hope of seeing a sign from Shining Star. But her magical pony had stayed away all night, and she'd seen only the stars twinkling and clouds skimming across the face of the full moon.

It was a grey, windy morning when Krista went outside to wave off her mum and dad then took her bike up the cliff path. Out to sea, a thick white fog lay low on the horizon.

Silver Mist

Krista pedalled hard. Her bike hit sharp rocks on the rough path and sent her skidding off course. Once, she almost lost her balance and fell against the barbed-wire fence between her and the cliff edge. She braked hard, dumped her bike in a gorse bush and ran the rest of the way.

Shining Star was waiting for her. He stood on the magic spot, breathing out a shimmering silver mist. When Krista arrived, he told her there was no time to lose.

Quickly she scrambled on to his back and waited for him to spread his wings. "Where are we going?" she asked.

"Back to Oakwood," he told her.

"Because of the woman in the car?"

My Magical Pony

"Partly. But also because there are trees there," Shining Star explained. "And when I hear the cries of the stolen horses, I see thick branches, a dark wood, and a secret place!"

Krista nodded. She trusted her magical pony to go where his "voices" led him.

With a rapid beat of his strong wings they rose from the ground. Once again Krista felt the earth whirl away beneath them as they flew. She saw nothing except a spinning tunnel of shadowy shapes, soon opening out into a silvery expanse.

Then she looked down and saw high walls and a grand house.

"Oakwood Hall!" Krista murmured, holding tight as usual while Shining Star swooped down towards the ground.

They landed behind the ancient house, in a meadow full of sheep, hidden from view by a hollow which led to a stream. Beyond the stream, Krista saw a hill sloping towards a thick wood, and beyond that the foggy sea.

"It feels creepy!" she muttered.

Shining Star walked to the edge of the stream and lowered his head to take a drink. Then he picked his way across the shallow water.

"I've never been here before," Krista told him.

My Magical Pony

She knew that Oakwood estate was private, with its own roads through the fields and wood. The people who lived in the house were very rich.

Steadily Shining Star walked down the hill towards the trees. As they approached, Krista saw how thickly they grew, with low branches almost touching the ground. "Are we going in there?" she asked in a scared voice.

"Yes, but you must get off and walk beside me," Star warned.

Reluctantly she slid down and they entered the shadow of the forest.

These were oak trees. Their trunks were old and twisted, their branches woven into a green canopy. Underfoot there was a thick layer of dry leaves that rustled as they walked.

"Can you hear anything?" Krista whispered to Shining Star.

He stopped, his head raised high, ears pricked. "Nothing," he said.

Disappointed, Krista glanced in every direction. Behind them she could still see daylight, but ahead the shadows deepened.

Then, to their surprise, two pinpricks of light appeared from the depths of the wood and the sound of a car engine broke the muffled silence.

Before Krista and Star had time to think, the car headlights shone full on them. It was too late to turn and run.

109

My Magical Pony

The Land Rover drew near along a rough track, then a man jumped out and strode towards them.

"How did you get in here?" he demanded, coming right up to Krista and casting an angry glance over her grey pony. "Don't you know this is private property?"

"We're lost!" Krista told him, scared by his loud voice. Dressed in a checked shirt, jodhpurs and riding boots, with dark hair and a thin face, it seemed that this might be the owner of Oakwood Hall.

"Did you find a way up the cliff from the beach?" the man went on angrily. "That's the only way into the estate. The rest is fenced off to stop trespassers."

Krista nodded but didn't say anything.

"Didn't you see the signs down there? They say 'Keep Out' in big red letters!"

"I'm sorry," she said. "We didn't mean to …"

"Yeah, whatever!" He cut her off, then called over to the Land Rover. "Don't worry, Hannah, it's just some stupid kid. I'll soon get rid of her!"

Inside the car. Krista caught sight of the blonde woman whom she'd seen twice before.

"Nick, it's the same one who was hanging

around here yesterday," the woman confirmed.

"Right, young lady, you and your pony are going to turn around and follow this track," the man ordered. "It runs through the estate, past the house and out of the main gate. Meanwhile, I'm going to get back into the car and follow you every step of the way."

"There's no need," Krista told him hastily. "We can find our own way out."

But he glared at her and showed that he wouldn't stand any argument. "Go!" he ordered. "And don't come back!"

"Why would that woman want lessons from Jo?" Krista demanded.

Silver Mist

She was riding Shining Star along the road out of town after the gates of Oakwood Hall had slid firmly shut behind them.

"I mean, that man called Nick was dressed in riding stuff. Surely the woman would ask him if she wanted to learn to ride!"

It wasn't the only thing that felt wrong. For instance, if these people had so much money, surely they would have their own horses. And had there been any need for the man to be quite so mad at them?

"He acted like they had something to hide!" Krista said to Star.

The pony agreed. "We should go back. But this time we must make sure that they don't see us."

Krista thought hard. "He talked about us coming up the cliff into the wood," she remembered. "There must be a back way in."

"Let's find it," Star said, taking a narrow turning towards the sea and following it until they came to a small, rocky cove on the shore.

Krista was glad that the tide was out, but worried by the thick sea mist that refused to clear. She looked around the pebbly beach backed by overhanging rocks, gazing up and wondering where to go from here.

"There are signs," Star said, trotting with Krista to the nearest one.

"Keep Out!" she read. "Private beach. No trespassers."

"This is Oakwood," Star decided. "Hold

tight." With a beat of his strong wings he came level with the cliff top. He landed lightly then told Krista to dismount.

Once standing, she looked ahead to the shadowy forest. From this side, all the trees leaned at an angle, constantly blown by the sea wind. Their branches skimmed the ground, trapping the wet mist and making the woods seem gloomier than ever.

"Now I hear the misery of the horses!" Shining Star declared. "It floats through the forest towards us."

And so, forgetting her fear of the dark shadows, Krista stepped forward, brushing against leaves, catching her foot in the twisting roots, feeling her way.

Silver Mist

It seemed, in the mist, that the trees were living things, reaching out with spiky fingers to touch her cheek. Their roots writhed up from the earth to trap her. High in their branches, small creatures moved.

Krista shuddered. Without Shining Star she wouldn't have found the courage to go on.

"Closer!" the magical pony whispered. "We are drawing near!"

At last she made out a solid shape amongst the ancient trees. It was a deserted stone building – broken down after years of disuse, with ivy creeping up its walls, and with great holes in the roof. "It's an old farm cottage!" she told Star.

"Did you hear that?" he murmured,

standing with his front legs braced as if ready to turn and flee.

Krista strained to hear. The cottage was shrouded in mist which curled around its walls and across an overgrown yard into a dark barn. She made out a high whinny – very faint and muffled. "Yes!" she cried. "I heard it!"

She wanted to rush forward, but Star stopped her. "It's not safe!" he warned.

But the idea that the horses were calling for help made Krista forget the danger. She sprang clear of the trees into the clearing surrounding the cottage and started to run through the fog.

The horse whinnied a second time. Krista

followed the sound, round the back of the cottage into the yard.

Then she stopped dead.

The man called Nick came out of the barn carrying a rope in one hand. He saw Krista and called over his shoulder. A second man appeared, leading a dark bay pony.

"Stand right where you are!" yelled the owner of Oakwood Hall.

First Krista recognized the pony. "Shandy!" she gasped. Then she identified the man who was leading her. It was Sean, the blacksmith!

The blacksmith quickly backed Shandy out of sight, closed a door and came back.

119

My Magical Pony

By this time, Shining Star had come up alongside Krista.

"You go for the pony. I'll get the girl!" Nick ordered, handing the rope to Sean. He ran towards Krista.

Scared to death, she stumbled to the front of the cottage, hearing Nick's footsteps close behind. A glance over her shoulder told her that Sean had used the rope to lash out at Star and drive him back.

"Don't do that!" Krista cried out and turned. She tried to duck her pursuer and run to help Shining Star. She saw the rope snake through the air again and land with a crack against the pony's back. She winced as Star rose on to his hind legs.

Silver Mist

"Got you!" Nick snarled, grabbing her round the waist from behind. She struggled as he lifted her off her feet.

"Leave Star alone!" she yelled.

Sean struck again. This time the rope whipped across the pony's neck. Star landed and was too slow to stop the attacker from looping the rope around his head. "OK, I've got the pony!" Sean shouted.

Then Nick turned and dragged Krista towards his Land Rover parked on a nearby track. The last she saw, before he flung her into the back and drove her away, was the sight of her wonderful magical pony, a rope around his neck, being dragged out of sight.

Chapter Eleven

Krista cowered on the floor of the Land Rover. She shook from head to foot at the horror of what had just happened.

Poor Shining Star! Remembering how the younger man had lashed out at him, Krista struggled to sit up. As she wrenched at the closed door and the driver set off down the dark track, Krista came to terms with the fact that Sean was one of the thieves.

I would never have guessed! she thought. *But it was definitely him!*

The Land Rover rocked and swayed over

the rough ground, throwing Krista back. But she could see daylight as they emerged from the woods, and she could tell that the driver was racing downhill towards the stream which she and Shining Star had crossed.

Krista held on to a metal ledge in the back of the car as it shot recklessly into the water. A cold spray rained down on her through an open window. Then there was a heavy thump as the Land Rover hit a rock, followed by the grinding of the engine. The tyres skidded in deep mud, and they came to a complete stop.

Krista seized her chance. She wrenched at the handle, and this time the door swung open.

The driver swore and tried to restart the engine.

My Magical Pony

Krista leaped out and ran – up the hill, across the field, back into the dark wood.

She ran faster than she had ever run before. She must save Shining Star and Shandy. She must find Scottie and Drifter!

Nick chased her. He shouted and swore.

Krista felt that he was gaining on her. She left the road and ran into the darkest shadows to throw him off her track.

But now she had to find her way to the old cottage, through the trees, ducking their branches and getting stuck in prickly under-growth. Still she could hear the man follow-ing her. He blundered through the leaves and bushes, breathing hard.

Silver Mist

Her throat was dry. Her legs felt weak as she jumped a ditch. She fell and rolled against a mossy log, then lay quiet as the man ran up and stopped almost directly above her. "Sean, I've lost the girl! Did she come your way?"

"I haven't seen her!" came the muffled reply.

And now Krista knew which way to go. Once her pursuer had taken off in another direction, she would follow the sound of Sean's voice, creeping slowly from tree to tree until the farm cottage came into view.

My Magical Pony

There it was, ghostly and silent in the mist.

Krista held her breath and edged forward, holding back when she saw a figure come out of the barn and stride down the track.

"Nick, where are you?" Sean shouted.

There was no reply.

"I don't like this!" the blacksmith yelled. "That kid's getting too close for comfort!"

Krista pressed herself against a tree trunk, praying that Sean and the man called Nick wouldn't spot her.

"Nick! I'm going to untie these horses, d'you hear me!"

Krista gasped.

"I'm going to let them go before she tells the police!"

Silver Mist

Still Sean yelled into a dark silence. Krista could hear the whinny of ponies, and then the sound of leaves rustling as Nick emerged on to the track.

"Don't be an idiot!" he shouted.

Krista peered around the tree trunk to see Sean run back into the long, low barn. Nick raced after him. She heard more angry voices and the high whinny of frightened horses.

Krista broke away from the shelter of the trees and ran towards the barn. She didn't care if the men saw her – all that mattered was to save Shining Star and the other horses.

"You're mad!" Nick cried, wrestling Sean to the ground as he unbuckled Shandy's head collar. The two men rolled across the floor.

Krista stood in the doorway, taking in the scene. In the darkness she made out a row of low pens, perhaps once used for sheep – but now each one contained a frightened horse.

She saw Shining Star, tied tightly to a metal ring in the wall. Then Shandy, loose in her stall, striking out with her front hooves. Scottie, his white blaze marked with a dark cut, his head hanging, then Drifter, and after that three more horses – no doubt the ones from Bay View.

Krista ran to untie Star.

"Are you all right?" she gasped. "Did he hurt you?"

"Not much," Star said, waiting patiently to be released.

Silver Mist

The stronger of the two men, Sean, wrenched himself free of Nick and sprang to his feet. "I'm getting rid of the evidence!" he yelled, ignoring Krista and working fast to release Scottie and then Drifter, before Nick seized him again and pulled him down.

Shandy, Drifter and Scottie reared and kicked. Their metal shoes raised sparks as they struck the stone walls. Struggling to escape, the three horses broke down the wooden walls of their stalls and made for the barn door.

"They're free!" Krista breathed. She pushed open the barrier that held Shining Star and together they followed the stolen horses.

*

"Scottie, don't be scared!" Krista pleaded in the grey mist of the cottage clearing.

The injured chestnut was wild with fear, his eyes rolling. He reared up and whirled away towards the dark wood.

"Shandy! Drifter!" she tried in vain to calm them.

Scottie reared again, then galloped for the cover of the trees. The two ponies charged after him.

"Come back!" Krista begged. They were

free from their prison, but in a frenzy, like wild horses. "Oh!" she cried in despair, turning to Shining Star. "How do we follow them?"

"Climb up," he ordered. He spread his wings and soared low over the oak trees.

Below them, Krista caught glimpses of the fleeing horses. She saw Scottie swerving between thick tree trunks, calling out to the two ponies. Then a sturdy, dark shape that must be Shandy, struggling out of a ditch, then Drifter following the sound of Scottie's call.

"Will they stop when they get tired?" Krista asked Shining Star.

"Not until they are safe," he replied. He circled overhead, keeping them in sight. Then he hovered. "Look ahead!" he warned.

My Magical Pony

Krista sensed a new danger. She could see the horses running on through the forest below, then realized with a dreadful shock that they were heading for the sea.

"Soon they will reach the cliff!" Shining Star told her.

"Surely they'll stop before then!"

He beat his wings and flew after them. "They are too afraid," he told her. "After days of being locked in that dark place, they can only think of escape."

Scottie thundered on through the woods, the smell of the sea in his nostrils and the promise of freedom ahead. Drifter and Shandy were close behind.

"How can we turn them away?" Krista said.

Silver Mist

The horses were only seconds from the cliff edge, galloping through the trees towards the light. With a beat of his great wings, Shining Star flew swiftly ahead of Scottie.

"Please stop!" Krista cried. She looked down at the dark, overhanging rocks and the dizzying drop into the sea.

Drifter galloped on, neck stretched, head straining forwards, towards the fatal fall.

"Stop them!" she pleaded with Shining Star.

Then her magical pony drew a deep breath and breathed out a fine silver mist. It sparkled as it fell to the ground, covering Scottie, Drifter and Shandy in a glittering cloud.

Krista watched as the magic mist worked its spell.

My Magical Pony

First Scottie breathed in the silver cloud. In an instant he came to a halt, letting the mist settle around him.

Then Drifter came alongside. He breathed deeply and was calm.

Finally, Shandy came under the glittering cloud. Steadily she looked down over the edge of the cliff and at the waves breaking in a white spray against the rocks.

Krista sighed. The ponies were safe!

Chapter Twelve

"This cut on Scottie's face will heal nicely now that we've cleaned it up," Krista's dad told her.

Krista held the chestnut's lead-rope as her dad worked with cotton wool and iodine. "Good boy!" she told him, resting her head against his cheek.

They stood in the yard at Hartfell. It was late Wednesday afternoon. Scottie, Drifter and Shandy were safe.

"That was a close thing," her dad went on, dabbing gently at Scottie's wound. "I just don't know how you and that little grey pony managed to turn them back from the cliff edge!"

"Me neither!" Krista murmured. How could she tell him that a magical silver mist had held them as if in a trance until she and Shining Star had flown for help?

"How long will they stay there?" Krista had asked as the flying pony had swooped across Whitton Bay and up to Hartfell.

"Until I release them," he'd told her.

Krista had waited for him to land on the top field, then gone running to tell her mum and dad that she'd found the stolen ponies.

Then everything had happened in a rush. Her dad had decided to drive Jo's spare horsebox to Oakwood and demand the return of Scottie, Shandy and Drifter. Meanwhile, Krista and Star had flown back to the woods and the cliff edge where they had left them.

"Amazing!" Krista had whispered when she had seen the ponies still standing like statues in the mist.

Shining Star had landed quietly. He had walked calmly from Scottie to Drifter and then to Shandy, nuzzling them and breathing over them until each had relaxed and returned to normal. The silver mist had gradually cleared.

Soon after, Krista's dad had driven up in the horsebox. "There's no sign of anyone at the house," he'd reported. "And the main gate was open."

My Magical Pony

Quickly they'd loaded the stolen horses into the box, then Krista had walked Star up the ramp and they'd all driven home.

"The danger is over." Shining Star told Krista as he prepared to leave.

"You're so cool!" she told him, a wide grin on her face. She stroked his silky mane.

"Where did that pony pop up from?" her dad wondered as he led Scottie up to the top field to join Drifter and Shandy. "He seems to have a knack of being around to help out when you need him."

Krista followed with Star beside her. "He wanders around the moor like the other wild ponies. I think he likes me!"

Silver Mist

Shining Star tossed his head and swished his tail.

"Here's your mum," her dad pointed out as their car drove up the lane. "Who's that in the car with her?"

"It's Rob!" she said, glancing with bright eyes at Shining Star.

Sure enough, Rob stepped out. "The police let me go!" he yelled, his arms spread wide. "They arrested Sean and the couple from Oakwood instead!"

"Apparently, Sean told them everything," Krista's mum explained. "They went over to his place the moment I drove into town and told them what had been going on. And guess what – they found Rob's trailer in Sean's garage."

"How come?" Krista asked.

"Rob has a deal with Sean to keep his trailer there. Sean claimed at first that Rob had taken it away and brought it back again without him knowing. But the police got the truth out of him in the end. He broke down and confessed everything."

"He said that the Oakwood couple had dragged him into a plan to steal the most valuable horses and ponies living around Whitton. Sean owed the couple money which he couldn't afford to repay, so he was forced to go in with them on the horse thefts. It was just a matter of luck that they chose to do the job at Jo's place on the one night when nobody was there keeping an eye on things."

"Huh!" Krista muttered. "So how come these Doyles needed to steal horses?"

"They've got money problems." Rob took over from Krista's mum. "They may live in a big house and look as if they've got loads of money, but the truth is, they owe the bank thousands. Stealing horses was a way to earn quick money, but it all went badly wrong."

"Or *right!*" Krista insisted. "I mean, in the end it went right for Scottie and the others!"

"Well, the Doyles certainly knew the value of a horse like Scottie," Krista's dad said. "It took someone with good knowledge to pick him out. I expect they thought Drifter would be worth plenty too."

"And I bet they stole Shandy because she loads so easily into a trailer and the other two would follow her."

Krista put her arm around Star's neck and said another quiet thank you.

Shining Star dropped his head and nuzzled her hand.

"All's well that ends well," Krista's dad concluded.

"And Jo was so pleased when we called to tell her that we'd got Scottie, Drifter and Shandy back!" Krista's mum added.

"You did? You rang her?" Krista gasped.

Her mum nodded. "Rob spoke to her."

Krista turned quickly to Rob. "Well?"

"Yeah, you could say she was relieved," he

grinned. "But not half as relieved as I was when the police said I could go, I can tell you!"

"And?" Krista insisted, her eyes shining as she crossed all her fingers. "What about Apollo? How did he get on?"

Rob folded his arms and put his head to one side. He frowned. Krista felt her high hopes drop like a stone.

"He came first!" Rob said with a quick grin.

"Oh ... wow!"

"First in the show-jumping and first overall," Krista's mum confirmed. "Jo's over the moon!"

"Perfect!" Krista sighed. "Isn't it – totally perfect?" she said to Shining Star.

Her dad laughed. "Talking to the animals again, Krista!"

My Magical Pony

As the grown-ups turned to walk down the lane towards the yard, Krista and Star stayed by the gate.

Krista glanced at Drifter, Shandy and Scottie quietly grazing. She sighed deeply and stroked her magical pony one last time.

"Goodbye, Krista," Shining Star whispered, breathing silver mist. He looked into her eyes with his soft dark gaze.

Then he spread his wings and flew away.